NINE STARSHIPS
WAITING

Hardcover ISBN 13: 978-1-5154-5933-0
E-Book ISBN 13: 978-1-5154-5934-7

NINE STARSHIPS WAITING

by Roger Zelazny

TABLE OF CONTENTS

NINE STARSHIPS WAITING

"The tiger is loose." it said.

He folded the message and placed it beneath a paperweight.

"You may go."

The man before him saluted sharply and did an about-face.

The Duke did not Look up.

He reached for a cigar and leaned back into his chair.

"The tiger is loose," he said, *"after all these years . . . "*

He lighted it and stared for a long while into the blue haze..

"I wonder what he'll look like, this time?"

MINUS TEN

He was awake.

For a long while he did not open his eyes. He thought of his arms and his legs and they were there. He tried to decide what he was, but he could not remember.

He began to shiver.

He felt a thin covering above his nude body. A draft of cold air was chilling his face.

He shook his head. Then he was on his feet, and dizzy.

He looked about.

A candle flickered on the table, beside a muddied skull. To the right lay a dagger.

He looked back at his bed. It was a coffin, the coverlet a shroud. Black-draped walls leaned toward him, the hangings gently a-rustle. There was a mirror on the farthest wall, but he did not feel like looking into it. There was no door.

"You are alive," said the voice.

"I know," he answered.

"Look into the mirror."

"Go to hell."

He stalked about the room, bunching the hangings together and tearing them loose, yards at a time. Ankle-deep in black velvet, he smashed the mirror.

"Pick up a piece of the mirror and look at yourself."

"Go to hell!"

"Do you know what you will see?"

He snatched the dagger from the table and began shredding the velvet into long ribbons.

"You will see a man," it continued, "a naked, useless man."

He hurled the skull across the room and it shattered against the wall.

"You will see a pitiful crawling worm, a hairless embryo, a fork of stripped willow; you will see a poor player, strutting and fretting . . . . "

He heaped the shredded cloth in the center of the cell and set fire to it with the candle. He pushed the table into the blaze.

"You know you are at the mercy of the elements you seek to control . . . . "

The hairs on his chest withered and curled. He glared upwards.

"Come down here," he invited, "whatsoever thou art, and this shall be thy pyre!"

Somewhere above him he heard a muffled click. The voice ceased. He threw his dagger high and it· struck metal.

It dropped back into the flames.

If I be so damned weak, what fearest thou?" he cried. "Come visit me in hell!"

The candle flickered out as a mist of fire foam descended. The bonfire persisted a moment longer, and the glowing table was last to vanish.

Silently, the nozzles in the wall sucked away his consciousness.

He fell across his coffin.

*

"How's he doing now, sir?"

"Mean as ever," said Channing.

The new Assistant Director studied the screen.

"Is he really everything they say?"

"Depends on what you've heard."

Channing adjusted the cell's thermostat to 68° Fahrenheit and switched on the recorder.

"If you've heard that he sank the Bismarck," he continued, "he did not. If you've heard that he assassinated Trotsky, he did not. He wasn't around then—but he thinks he was, and he thinks he did. But if you think that New Cairo vanished in a natural disaster, or that General Kenton died of food poisoning, you're wrong."

The new Assistant shuddered and unhooked an earphone. He listened to the words broadcast at the anesthetized- man.

" . . . You are death and damnation in human form. You are the lightning of Nemesis attracted by mortal rods. You assassinated Lincoln. You killed Trotsky —split his skull like a melon. You pulled the trigger at Sarajevo and smashed the seals of the Apocalypse. You are the poisoned blade that bled the Court of Denmark, the bullet in Garfield, the steel in Mercurtio—and the fires of vengeance burn in your soul forever.—You are Vindici, the son of Death . . . . "

It droned on and on, in a flat matter-of-fact tone. The Assistant Director hung the earphone back on the board and looked away from the Gothic setting on the screen.

"You fellows are rather thorough about these things, aren't you?"

Channing snorted what might pass for a chuckle.

"Thorough?" he asked. "He is the only complete success we've ever had. Over the past nineteen years he has been responsible for more mayhem than any tidal wave or earthquake in history."

"Why all the rhetoric?"

"He's a character out of a play."

The Assistant shook his head and shrugged.

"When can I talk to him?"

"Give us three more days," answered Channing. "It's still feeding time."

*

Cassiopeia looked up from her balcony at the four new stars. On another planet, which she had never visited, a similar formation would have been called the Southern Cross. The constellation above her bore no name, however, and the four points of the cross had once blazed from man-made hearths on four separate worlds.—Steel rood of the forges, its arms did not wink like stars.

Gray-eyed, she watched till they were out of sight. Turning, green-eyed, she entered her apartments, with hair of tiger gold and cloak of tiger black.

And she wondered, behind her changing eyes—Who would come to tear down the cross over Turner's World?

When she thought she knew she cried herself to sleep.

MINUS NINE

The world of Stats' a drunken bat;
It woggles to and fro.
How it avoids the asteroids,
Only God and the Statmen know.
And who it was that writ these lines
Where the cool flush tank flows,
And why he cannot leave this place,
Only Statcom knows.
—Carl Smythe, Sp. Asst. Dr. Channing, identity determined Statcom Code 11-7, Word Order Analysis.

*

Is he coherent yet?"

"If you mean will he understand you, yes. The term 'coherency,' however, does not apply."

"What do you mean?"

"His mind is not a coherent whole in any psychiatric sense. He is two personalities—one aware only of itself, and the other of both selves."

"Schizoid?" the Assistant Director asked, matter of factly.

"No. Neo-Kraepelinian typology doesn't apply."

"Which one will I be talking to?"

"The one we need."

"Oh."

Smythe, who had been rummaging in a drawer, turned to them with a grin. He caressed a laser-gun the size of an automatic pencil, then slipped it into his breast pocket.

"You won't be needing that," said the Assistant Director. He reached behind his belt and withdrew a compact pistol.

"Small, but deadly," he smiled.

"Yes, I know," said Channing. "Give it to me."

"What do you mean 'give it to you'? I'm going to be talking to a psychopathic killer. I want a gun of my own."

"The hell you say! You're not going in there with that thing!"

With grizzled crewcut, patches of scalp showing through, porcine features, and his short, stocky build, Doctor Karol Channing resembled nothing so much as a razorback hog.

He held forth a wide hand.

The Assistant dropped his eyes, then placed his gun in the outstretched palm.

"Since Smythe is armed, I guess it's all right . . . . "

Channing grinned.

"He's not *your* bodyguard."

"Smythe! Damn it! I want a drink!"

"You're leaving tomorrow, Vindici. Do you want a big head when the hyper-drive cuts in?"

"Damn the h.d.! and damn my head tomorrow! It's my stomach I'm thinking of now!" A wheedling note crept into his voice. "Be a good fellow and fetch us a bottle."

Smythe's freckled face twisted, then split.

"Okay, dad, it's your frame. You're my charge till you leave, and keeping you happy is part of the job description. Hold the fort, I'll be back."

Smythe ducked out the door of the apartment and Vindici noted with pleasure that he did not lock it behind him. He shook his head. Why should that thought have occurred to him? He was no prisoner. He crossed to the mirror and studied himself.

A little under six feet, a little underweight—but that always happens in the sleep tanks—black hair with flecks of white at the temples, mahogany eyes, straight nose, firm chin.

The man in the mirror wore an expensively-cut gray jacket and a light blue shirt.

He rubbed his eyes. For a moment the reflection had been blond and green-eyed, with fuller lips and darker skin.

He raised the water tumbler between the thumb and index finger of his delicate right hand. He squeezed until it shattered. The pieces fell into the bowl.

He smiled back at his reflection.

The door opened behind him and Smythe entered with an almost-full fifth of Earth bourbon and two glasses.

"Good thing you brought an extra glass. I just broke mine."

"Oh? Where is it?"

"In the bowl. Bumped it."

"I'll clean it out. That," frowned Smythe, "is also in my job description."

Vindici smiled mechanically and filled both glasses. He downed his in a gulp and refilled it.

Smythe dumped the shards into the disposal slot.

"How you feeling?" he said.

Vindici added ice, then took another drink.

"Fine—now?"

Smythe finished washing his hands and dropped into a chair.

"Damn' I cut myself!"

Vindici chuckled.

"Blood!"

He sighed, and continued,

" . . . The most beautiful thing in the universe, cloistered in the darkest places possible and blushing most admirably when exposed."

*

Smythe wrapped it in his handkerchief, hastily.

13

"Yeah. Sure."

"Furthermore " said Vindici.

"Have you got all the typography straight?"

"Yes, I used to live there."

"Hm. Well—"

"Yes. I did live there, didn't I? Or was it Captain Ramsay?—Sure, Turner's Guard. He was an officer."

"That's right, but that was long ago. I was a kid."

Vindici took another drink.

"And I'm going to kill someone. I won't know who until I get there. But I wanted to kill—someone—then—"

He looked at Smythe.

"Do you know why I'm going?"

"Nope. I'm just the garbage man."

He passed his hand before his eyes.

"That's not true," he said. "I see a centaur . . . . You are a man from the waist up and a bank of machinery below . . . . "

Smythe laughed nervously.

"My girl back home would be surprised to hear that—don't tell her. But seriously, why are you going?"

Vindici shook his head.

"Eagles over Nuremberg."

"Huh?"

"Starships—battle conches—are gathering at Turner's World."

Smythe shrugged.

"What do we care if they take the place? In fact, it would be a good idea."

The dark man shook his head.

"They're not there to take the place."

Smythe halted his drink in mid-movement.

"Oh. How often have we smashed Turner's World?" he mused. "At least three times in the past sixty years. Won't they ever give up?"

Vindici's chuckle made him check to see whether he had swallowed one of his ice cubes.

"Why should they?" asked the other. "The Fed would never sanction out-and-out destruction of Turner's World. It might make too many neutrals cease being neutral. So they just de-fang it every twenty years or so."

"One day," he smiled, "the dentist will arrive too late."

"What's your part in all this? You're a Turnerian, you fought the Federation . . . ."

"I'm the dentist," growled Vindici, "and I hate the place! It's a violation of Fed Code to station more than two conches within five light years of one another. A world can only own a maximum of two."

"And Turner's World has none—Article Nine of the last war settlement," supplied Smythe, "but they can quarter two."

"Four have already arrived," said Vindici. "Six would constitute a first class Emergency. Statcom says there will be at least seven."

Smythe gulped his drink.

Six conches could destroy six worlds, or hold them. At least six words . . . .

"From where?" he asked.

"The Pegasus, from Opiuchus—the Stilleto, from Bran the Stand back, from Deneb and the Minotaur."

"Then the Graf Spee and the Kraken may be on their way."

Vindici nodded.

"That's what Statcom thinks."

"Could a simple assassination stop them?"

"Statcom thinks so—but an assassination is never simple. I may have to kill the whole High Command, whoever they are."

Smythe winced.

"Can you do it?"

Vindici laughed.

"That world killed me once, which was a mistake. They should have let me live."

Then they killed the bottle, and Smythe hunted up another. As they became the hub of the galaxy, with lopsided universes spinning about them,

Smythe remembered asking, "Why, Vindici? Why are you the weapon that walks like a man?"

The next morning he could not remember the answer, except that part of it was an Elizabethan monologue delivered to an empty bottle, beginning, "My study's ornament, thou shell of death . . . and punctuated with numerous "'sblud's," before the man had collapsed, sobbing, across the bedstead—and he could not find him to say goodbye. because Vindici had blasted off at 0500 hours, for Turner's World. But it did not really matter to Smythe.

MINUS EIGHT

Are you the one?"

"Yes."

"Name me the place."

"Stat."

"Name me the time."

"Any."

"Come in."

Vindici entered quickly and surveyed the room. It held the normal furnishings of a provincial hotel, untouched, save for a heaped ashtray.

Vindici inspected the closet and the small washroom.

"There's no one under the bed either."

Vindici looked.

"You're right."

He eyed the slender man with the nervous tic and the hair too dark for what there was of it.

"You're Harrison,"

He nodded.

"You're Vindici."

He smiled.

"I've come to kick those four stars out of the sky before they have puppies. What's the word?"

"Sit down."

"I can listen standing up!'

Harrison shrugged. He seated himself.

"Turner's World has always been the catalyst. The Opiuchuans and the Denebians are ready. The Eighth Reich will have two conches here by tonight. They don't trust each other, but they've agreed upon Duke Richard as command—"

"Richard!" Vindici took a step forward, hands raising.

Harrison stared into his eyes, unmoving, except for the left corner of his mouth which jerked like the wing of a moth.

Finally, he nodded.

"Richard de Tourne. He's old, but he's still vicious and cunning."

Vindici spat upon the carpet and stamped on it. A slow metamorphosis began to unwind his saturnine features.

His cheekbones lowered and his lips began to swell, the streaks of white at his temples grew yellow.

"Your eyes!" Harrison exclaimed. "They're changing, Vindici!"

The man shrugged off the jacket which had grown too tight across his shoulders. He threw it the length of the room.

"Who's Vindici?" he asked.

*

Fifty cubic miles of steel and plastic, like a quarterback running a broken field, Stat.

Steel dancing through blizzards of rock, with an infallible pilot, Statcom.

Statcom, charting possible futures and their remedies. Stat did not exist, because Statcom had debunked the rumors of itself two generations ago. Fed had no weapon for first class Emergencies other than diplomacy or military force—Statcom had said so.

Channing found Smythe in the Armory of Forbidden Weapons, fondly studying a 1917 trench knife.

"He's arrived," said Channing.

The lanky redhead replaced the knife on the rack.

"Why tell me?"

"Thought you might like to know."

"Meet Harrison yet?"

"Should have."

"Good. Thanks to your work he is now Captain Ramsay, which is even better than being Vindici, for the moment."

"Sir?"

A long second passed as Smythe studied the trench knife.

"Statcom said you'd guess sooner or later today. It didn't pinpoint the hour, though."

"I know. I asked it after I figured things out."

"Congratulations, you've just won yourself a free brainwash and an all-expense trip home."

"Good, I hate this place."

"When did you learn?"

"I've suspected you were the Director for some time now, You've always protested more loudly then anyone else about conditions here. You tipped your hand, though, by having Statcom override sound therapy and recommend that you get drunk with Vindici. You always were fascinated by weapons."

"I'll have to watch that in the future," laughed Smythe, "and I'll have Statcom chart the periodicity of my complaints. You always were pretty sharp when it came to minds, though—human or mechanical."

"Which are you?"

"I'm a part of Stat," he answered, "and I'm writing history before it happens, in a book no one will ever read and tell of—author unknown."

"You're mad," said Channing.

"Of course. I'm drunk as Dionysus, and dedicated as the three old women with the spinning wheels—and as omnipotent. When you return to your quarters the medmen will be waiting."

Channing eyed the rack of knives.

"I could kill you right now, if I had a little more cause. But what you're doing may be right. I just don't know."

"I know," answered Smythe, "and you never will."

Channing's shoulders sagged.

"What part will my poor imposter play in all this?"

"The most difficult of all, of course—himself."

Smythe turned his back and studied a gigantic Catalan knife.

"Go to hell," muttered Channing.

He might have heard a metallic chuckle as he left the Armory.

MINUS SEVEN

And you don't think he'll recognize you?" asked Harrison.

"With a white beard and a bald dome? I'm dead, remember?"

"Richard isn't senile—and he'll probably be expecting something like this."

"I'll be working for his son, Larry. He was an infant the last time I saw him. Richard won't even see me, until the last thing."

Ramsay looked across the great courtyard. A square mile of lush vegetation, an artificial lake, a row of summer cottages, and a small menagerie lay beneath him. Servants were clearing the remains of an all night party from about a huge pavilion. Broken dishes were confetti upon the grass, and pieces of cloth decorated the branches of trees. Slow-moving men with rubbish sacks were insects far below, gathering up everything in sight. The greenly lowering sun was balanced like a gigantic olive atop the forty-foot wall which enclosed the estate.

Something came loose at the bottom of his brain.

"Where have I been all this time? It seems so very long since I lived in the officers' quarters, there," he pointed, "across the lake. Was I very ill?"

"The sleep," said Harrison. "It was long. There was no antidote for the poison Richard used, so your friends put you in the sleep tanks until one could be developed."

"How long was I out?"

"Nineteen years."

Ramsay closed his eyes and touched his forehead. Harrison clapped him on the shoulder.

"Don't think about it now. Your mind is still recovering from the shock. You want to get this thing over with first, don't you?"

"Yes, that's right I do. Larry is a man now . . . . "

"Of course—a baby wouldn't be hiring a pimp, would he?"

Ramsay laughed, and his eyes matched the color of the sun.

"A pimp! How royal! How grand and fitting!"

His laughter became demented. It rolled and echoed about the high hall. Harrison coughed loudly.

"Perhaps you had better uh—compose yourself. He'll be here soon, and you should be properly subservient."

He sobered, but a smile continued to play about the corners of his mouth.

"All right. I'll spend the next five minutes thinking of money and sex. I'll save this for later—"

His right hand darted behind his back and up beneath the hem of his jacket.

Simultaneously, there was a blurring movement and a click.

Harrison looked cross-eyed at the switch blade touching his Adam's Apple. He licked his lips.

"Excellent form—but please put it away. What if Larry were to walk in here and see—?"

"Then this would happen," he replied, without moving his lips.

The blade was gone again.

"Very impressive." Harrison swallowed half of the last word.

"It will stay put now, until bleeding time."

They lighted cigarettes and waited.

*

The door finally opened, soundlessly, behind Ramsay. He turned, nevertheless, smirking at the thin-faced boy who stood upon the threshold.

The youth looked through him and into Harrison.

"Is he the man?"

"He is."

"What's his name?"

"Pete."

"Pete, I'm Leonard de Tourne, first heir of this damned amusement park." He walked past them and hurled himself into an easy chair so hard that it banged against the wall. He wiped his moist forehead on a silken sleeve and crossed his legs. His dark eyes focused on Ramsay. "I want a woman," he announced.

Ramsay chuckled out loud.

"That's easily accomplished."

The boy ran many-ringed fingers through his thatch of unruly black. He shook his head.

"No, it isn't. I want *a* woman, not just any woman."

"Oh, a special transaction."

"That's right, and the price is no object."

Ramsay rubbed his chemically-wrinkled hands together.

"Good! Good! I like challenges—and big commissions."

"You'll be well paid."

"Excellent! What's her name?"

"Cassiopeia."

The green-gray eyes squinted.

"Unusual name."

"She's the human daughter of two dead halfies, and very beautiful. Her father was part native and her mother was an orphan from God knows where. When they're fertile, those hybrid types produce either lovely children or freaks—or lovely freaks.

"Her mother was a servant girl named Gloria," he finished, "and her father was an officer in the Guard—I forget his name."

Ramsay nodded, then looked away.

"Where does she live?"

"In an apartment building in town. She owns it. Both parents died at the same time, and my father endowed the child. I don't know why."

"Give me the address and I'll see her directly."

NINE STARSHIPS WAITING

"Good." His lips curved into a half-smile and he pulled a wrinkled envelope from his pocket.

"That's the address on the outside. Inside is money."

Ramsay opened it and counted.

"She must be very desirable."

"Use as much as you have to, and keep the rest for your fee. I want her this week—tonight, if possible. I'll give you a note so that you can come and go as you choose, in this part of the palace. But don't try to cross me! The world isn't big enough for anyone to hide from a Tourne."

Ramsay bowed, very low. His voice wavered and, for a moment, held Vindici's deep resonance.

"True to my profession, m'lord—I have never failed an assignment."

*

The moon hurled down spears of silver. The six racing stars darting between them were a three-headed dragon with a long tail.

Cassiopeia looked away.

The tiger's tread was on the stair behind her violet eyes. *In the marble garden of Medusa Perseus sleeps in stone . . .*

MINUS SIX

General Comstock stared at the purple-veined nose, then shifted his gaze to the tip of Richard's cigar.

"They may try to assassinate you . . . " he began.

"Not 'may'," corrected the Duke. "'Will.'"

The Denebian's eyes widened.

"You have heard a rumor?"

The Duke shook his head and passed him the message he had received earlier.

"Not a rumor," he stated, "a fact. Stat is sending Vindici."

Comstock tugged his goatee and read the brief sentence.

"I didn't think Stat really existed."

"Fed has done a good coverup job—good enough to fool anyone. But I know that Stat exists because I know Vindici exists."

"I'll buy Stat," said Comstock, handing back the note, "but not Vindici. When it comes to superman, there's just no such animal. Heroes, yes. Lucky fools, yes. But don't try to sell me a superman."

"This is my last strike at the Federation," said Richard, after a long pause. "Win, loose, or draw, I die. The tiger is here on Turner's World and it's just a matter of time because I killed him when he was only a man."

"Killed?"

"Killed. Stat knew what he was then, and my failure to keep him dead gave them the tiger. After an hour and a half they dragged him back from hell, and

25

a man named Channing created Vindici from what was left."

"What was he then?"

"A halfy. A genuine, fertile halfy." He touched the saint's ikon on hill desk. "A soulless cross between humanity and a Turnerian native."

"They're telepaths, aren't they?"

Richard shrugged.

"Some' are, others are other things. But no one knows what a man like Channing could do with the mind of a broken halfy—Channing certainly doesn't know."

"Doctor Karol Channing, the Adler of the twenty-third century! Is he your man?"

"Of course. Who do you think sent this message? He's a sympathizer, but like most academicians he won't go overboard for revolution. He doesn't even know where Stat is, anyhow. All he did was send me a message that I'm going to die."

"This place is built like Fed's gold vault."

"So was Kenton's HQ."

Comstock crushed out his cigarette in the huge pewter tray.

"It's been rumored that he didn't really die of food poisoning. But still, the man took chances."

"Everyone takes chances—like walking up a flight of stairs, like eating food. The tiger is quite real, he's here in Cyril, and I have no idea what he looks like. It's been close to nineteen years since I've seen him. And halfies can change shape," he added.

"Just supposing he succeeds," asked Comstock, "have you any plans?"

"My son, Larry, can take over. You make the decisions, and he'll supply the name of Tourne. He's been briefed."

"Very well, then that's settled. Can I lend you some bodyguards?"

The Duke's ruddy cheeks expanded with his chuckle.

"When you leave, go through the North Wing. Stop in the main dining room and look at the wall."

"What's there?"

"Three words, in red chalk."

"All right. I'll take these maps with me. I'll be back this afternoon."

"Good morning."

The General saluted and Richard returned it. The metal doors slid open, soundlessly. He walked past them and his bodyguards headed toward the North Wing.

"Tonight," said Richard, "in Samarkand."

*

Good morning, my lovely. You have not changed.—Here, in the tombs of ice, time does not wither . . . Only . . . Only that green mark of the kiss that stops the heart . . . . Gloria! I'm going to see our daughter. That human puppy of Tourne wants her.—What's that?—No, of course not. But I must see her. I'd imagine she looks like you.—She is either lovely, or a lovely freak, he said. Like mother, like daughter, they say, and like father like son.—Richard killed us when you threw the wine in his face, but I'm back.—Smashed form releases chaos; chaos smashes other forms—rebound! The puppy wants her, as the dog wanted you, my fairest bitch.—Save your tears of ice. I'll reap two souls, and root the tree of Turner!—No! Wait for me.—Save your icy spit for the souls of Tournes, when they face you—not far removed, but near . . .

"Good-bye, my lovely."

MINUS FIVE

Pete?"

"Yes, my lord?"

"I understand that my son hired you because of your—er—profession."

"That's right, sir."

"I'm, well, I'm rather tense. Do you know what I mean?"

"No, sir."

"Hell! You're as old as I am! You know the feeling."

"Sir?"

"Dammit! I've got an itch for a woman and I want to be fixed up! Is that plain enough?"

"Very clear."

"Good. Here's something for your trouble. Get me a young one."

"Where shall I bring her?"

"That furthermost summer cottage will be deserted." He pointed out the window. "Tonight, say eleven o'clock?"

"She'll be there with bells on."

"Heh! I'd prefer a little less."

"Naked to the bone, my lord?"

"Not quite that far. Heh!"

"True to my profession, m'lord."

*

Rather than take the elevator, he climbed nine flights of stairs. When he

29

reached her door he paused. It opened.

"Oh. I didn't know there was anyone . . . "

"I was about to knock."

"I must have heard you on the stair."

"Must have."

She stood aside and he walked into the apartment, etching each painted screen, each grass mat and low table on the metal plate at the bottom of his mind.

"Won't you sit down?"

"Thank you."

He fumbled for the envelope.

"You are Cassiopeia Ramsay?"

"Yes."

"I've come from the Court of Tourne."

She stared into the Alcatraz of his eyes. Dreamlike, the words passed between them as they watched each other, waves matching colors on a sunny sea.

"Leonard, the son of Richard, desires your presence in his chambers. Tonight, if possible."

"I see. What will happen?"

Nothing.

"He wants to sleep with you."

"Oh. And you are the royal—factotum?"

Why will nothing happen?

"Yes, and well paid. I've brought you much money also. Here."

He will be dead.

"Very well, I'll be there. What time?"

"Say midnight."

"Midnight," she smiled.

Midnight.

When he left the seas became Chianti, and overflowing.

But Perseus of the glacier arm, sword of ice . . . The sun is burning bright!

Then, for the first time in many years, she laughed.

*

Comstock's Commandos laced the darkness. A tug, and their lines would tighten.

Anyone could enter. Nothing could leave.

"You got the time, Al?"

"Ten till."

Soot-barrelled laser rifles protruding through ink-dipped fronds . . . .

"Think anyone'll come?"

"Naw."

Fractional wattage; dim cottage, still.

"What if Richard decides to take a walk?"

"Don't be the man he spots. Comstock's out on a limb."

"Cripes, it's the old man's neck! He oughta be grateful."

"It's not his order, so shut up."

Stark, and the static of insects . . . .

"Who's that in the cottage?"

"Dunno. So long as no one comes out it don't matter."

"If they do?"

"We observe."

Moist wind, the laughter of thunder . . .

"You bring a poncho?"

"Yeah, didn't you?"

"Damn!"

Footsteps.

*

Through jagged intermittences of the Belt Stat sucked weightless quantities: words, from everywhere.

Three times a day Statcom took thirty-second vacations from heavier matters and translated everything into mantalk—millions of units of mantalk. Then it placed everything into categories of importance.

When the Code-V prefix appeared, it dropped all the other words into screaming heaps in its Pend-drum and uttered lights the color of sucked cinnamon drops.

The long tongue of paper rattled at Smythe. He ceased his manicuring and poked the nail-file through it.

Raising it, he read.

Smiling, he let it fall again.

Having informed the forebrain that Ramsay was about to die, the cerebellum returned to chewing its cud.

The cerebrum focused its attention on a thumbnail.

*

". . . Palsy and ague," answered Ramsay, "that's what's happening. Scream if you wish—no one will hear you."

"Dead. She is dead," said Richard.

"Of course. You made her that way, nineteen years ago. Remember?"

Ramsay put an arm around the delicate shoulders. He turned the seated woman, slowly.

"Gloria? Do you remember Gloria?"

"Yes. Yes! I do! My throat is burning!"

"Excellent I Wait till it hits your lungs!"

"Who are you? You couldn't be—"

"But I am!"

His eyes blazed orange, and he raised his arms over his head. Like leaves, the years fell away.

"Captain Ramsay—Vindici!"

"Yes, it's Ramsay," he told him. "I was going to use a knife, but this way is better. You wanted to kiss her so badly a moment ago—years ago. Badly enough to kill her and her husband."

The Duke began to gag.

"Be quick about your dying. I must return her to the vaults and finish another job."

"Not my son!" he choked.

"Yes, old man old—filthy, rotten poisoner—and for the same reason. You to my wife, he to my daughter—and father and son in double harness to hell!"

"He is young!" he cried out.

"So was Gloria. And so Cassiopeia . . . . "

The Duke screamed, one long blade of a howl, broken off at the end.

Ramsay looked away, mopping his forehead.

"Die, damn you! Die!"

"Green lipstick," muttered Richard. "Green lipstick . . . . "

The walls splintered about them, Ramsay whirled like a bat passing through the blades of a fan. He chopped the first man he saw, across the throat. He snatched his rifle and began firing.

Three men fell.

He leapt across a body and stepped through the exploded wall, firing first to his left and then to his right.

A rifle butt caught him in the back and he dropped to his knees.

Heavy boots began kicking at his kidneys, his ribs.

He curled into a ball, his hands clasped behind his neck.

Before everything disappeared he saw a candle, a skull, a dagger, and a mirror.

*

Hello," she said.

"Hello yourself. You're early."

"A few minutes."

"Couldn't wait, eh?"

"You might say that."

He walked around her, studying. He patted her hips.

"You're going to be all right, girl. God! Your eyes! I've never seen eyes that color."

"They change," she told him.

"This is my happy color."

He smirked, then touched her hair, her cheek . . . .

"Well, let's get real happy."

He pulled her to him, fumbling for the clasps at the back of her dress.

33

"You're warm," he said, pushing the straps off her shoulders. "Real warm." Without releasing her, he leaned back and turned off the main light.

"Makes things more cozy. Me, I like atmosphere—What was that?"

"A scream," she smiled.

He pushed her away and ran to the window.

"Must have been some damned bird," he said after awhile.

She shrugged off the rest of her clothing and stood swaying in the dim light, with hair of tiger gold and penetrating eyes of tiger black . . . .

"That was the Duke, your father," she told him, softly. "You have just succeeded to the title.

Long live Duke Larry!—at least till midnight."

He turned, his back against the sill.

"Take a long, last look. The vaults of ice are lonely."

He tried to scream, but her body was a sheet of white flame and her eyes were two black suns; he stared like a wild thing trapped.

She did not move, and he could not.

The ivory furniture of fascination, her shoulders, and the two blue-lined moons, her breasts, floated on that river of ballads, her tiger hair, inside his head; then everything twisted in icy waves of paralysis about the tree of his spine, until it became a frozen sapling.

"Halfy!" he choked, before it seized him completely.

MINUS FOUR

Is he going to live?" asked the fat sergeant.

"Don't know yet," answered the tall one, wiping egg from his mustache. "As soon as they give him new blood it becomes tainted. They can't transfuse fast enough to dilute it. Lungs are paralyzed. They've got a squeeze-box on his chest, and he's doped up plenty."

"Who takes over if he dies?"

"The kid, they say."

"God!"

He looked at the figure on the cot. The man blinked up at the ceiling and did not move. Four of Comstock's Commandos sat at the points of the compass with weapons pointed in his direction.

"What about him?"

"We're going to question him as soon as he comes to his senses."

"He's the tiger?" he asked.

"That's what they say."

"He'd know about Stat then."

"That's right."

The fat man's high-pitched voice shook. His small, dark eyes gleamed.

"Let me question him!"

"Everybody wants to. What's so special about you?"

"He tried to kill the Duke. I have the same dibs as anyone else."

The other shook his head.

"We're going to draw straws for the first session. You'll have the same chance as the rest of us."

"Good." The fat man hitched up his belt. "I want a tiger's tooth bracelet."

*

Richard lay encased in the coffin of coils, tubes, diaphragms, and bottles. It breathed for him. It did the work of a hundred pairs of kidneys. It charged his blood with vitamins and antiserums. It prodded his reticulo-endothelial system into storms of protest.

He thought for himself, however, during the strange periods of calm through which his mind drifted. It was as if he were free of his burning flesh and floating bodiless in empty space . . . .

Youth's the season made for joy. Love is then a duty . . .

Snatches of old songs pursued him. He felt peacefully impotent for the first time since his childhood.

A flash of remorse illuminated his inner night as he thought of the Federation—the slow-turning, in-gathering, chewing, digesting Federation. The Turnerian Axis was the last great opposition to its octopal embrace. Vanishing, like memories of his youth, the autonomy with which the frontier worlds had once been endowed, into the maw of the octopus—its movements seeking to emulate the wheel and spin of the galaxy—to become cells of the beast.

No! He would not let it happen. He would live! All nine starships had arrived and were waiting, somewhere above, in a V-formation. Nine starships waiting for his hand to guide their spear into the eye of the octopus, and down through its heart, Stat! He tried as hard as he could to live,

The feelings of fire returned.

*

"You can't hold me forever, halfy!" he gasped. "You're losing your grip already!"

"That's right," she smiled.

"Someone will come to tell me what that commotion was—they will find you here . . . . "

"No," she said.

" . . . Then you're going to wish. you had never been born,"

"I've been doing that for nineteen years," she answered, before breaking a vase on his head.

Old father, old artificer, what has happened?

I've failed.

Vindici does not fail.

Who is Vindici?

You must try to remember . . .

*

"I win!" giggled the fat man.

Tiger, tiger . . .

"I win," he repeated.

Burning bright . . .

"I'll use that room," he pointed.

I'm coming.

"Go ahead."

Get out of the palace.

He arose, and the guards dragged Ramsay to his feet.

Do you remember?

They pushed him in the direction of the storage room.

I'm trying. Get out of the palace!

He staggered forward and lurched against the wall.

Why?

The door swung open, Many hands pushed him, and he was inside the room.

I don't know. But I know that you must leave now.

He stayed on his feet, with effort. He stood in the center of the room, squinting puffy eyelids to shield his yellow-gray stare from the naked bulb overhead.

There are nine star-ships in the sky . . . .

Go home!

The sergeant smiled and closed the door behind him. He locked it, placed the key in his pocket.

"So you're the tiger. You don't look so fierce."

Ramsay shook his head and glared.

The sergeant removed the gun from his belt and slipped it behind his waistband. Slowly, luxuriating in each movement, he unclasped his wide leather belt and drew it from around his waist. He began wrapping it about his right hand.

Tiger, tiger . . .

When only the buckle and two inches of leather extended from his fist he smiled and took a slow step forward.

Burning bright . . .

Ramsay reached over his head and broke the lightbulb.

"Better yet, Vindici," came the chuckle.

The fat man took three steps through the blackness, toward the place where Ramsay stood.

In the forest of the night . . .

He raised his right hand to strike.

What immortal hand or eye dare frame . . .

The second last sound that he heard was a metallic click from behind his back. Something seized a handful of his hair and a knee jammed into his spine.

He felt something, like a piece of ice, touch his throat, and he was suddenly very wet.

The last sound that he heard was either a gurgle or a soft laugh or both.

*

Comstock sprang to his feet, face whitening.

"Escaped?"

"Yes sir," writhed the lieutenant.

"Who is responsible?"

"Sergeant Alton." The lieutenant was chewing his lower lip.

"Have him shot immediately."

"He's already dead, sir. Vindici cut his throat and took his gun. He killed five guards. There was an open window and one missing uniform."

"Find him. Bring him here if you can. If you can't, then bring me what's left."

"Yes, sir. We're searching now."

"Get out of here! Help find him!"

"Yessir."

A memory nagged him for a long moment. Then he seated himself and raised the comm lever.

"Sir?"

"Double Richard's guard. That man is loose again."

He dropped the lever without waiting for a reply.·

"He was right," he told the empty screen. "He was really right."

*

The world of Stat's a drunken bat, It woggles to and fro . . .

*

"He's failed," Harrison told the shiny brown box.

"Is he still alive?" it asked.

"Yes, but—"

"Then he hadn't failed," it answered.

"But he'll be dead soon . . . . "

There was a sound like the breaking of strings on a steel guitar.

Harrison realized then that he was talking to himself.

He closed the box, his mouth, and his mind, and went to join the tiger hunt.

*

—Father . . .

—Who is that?

—Cassy, but . . .

—I know no one named Cassy. I am no one's father.

—You are Vindici. You are also Captain Ramsay. I am your daughter.

—I borrow Ramsay occasionally. You are his daughter, not mine.

39

—Very well, have it your way. But look above you.

—I am underground. There is nothing to see.

—There are nine starships in the sky, waiting to strike at the Federation.

—They won't get that far.

—Perhaps I want them to.

—Why?

—We both have reason to kill Richard. But the Federation . . . Perhaps there is reason to break it also.

—What reason?

—It has already served its purpose. It's gotten man to the stars. Now it is a huge sponge, sopping the blood of worlds that cry for independence. Squeeze it, and it will shrink; bleeding . . . .

—That's not my job.

—Once it was my father's. Long ago.

—And Richard killed him! Are you suggesting that Richard's plan be permitted to proceed, unaltered?

—Only you know where Stat is located . . . .

—That's right.

—Do you remember Gloria?

Silence.

—Men ahead! Lights!

Flight, wordless.

Hate, an active verb.

Fury, the inside of a furnace.

Pain—

Silence . . . .

MINUS THREE

He was awake.

For a long while he did not open his eyes. He thought of his arms and his legs and they were there. He tried to decide what he was, but he could not remember.

He began to shiver.

Then the pain came.

He had been running, running through passages under the ground. He stirred the bonfire of memory. He had been working his way beneath the palace. He was nearing the huge vents. Someone had been talking to him, from somewhere.

The bonfire smouldered.

Someone, probably Ramsay, had wanted him to smash Stat. He remembered killing many men. He remembered being backed against the wall, his gun snatched away. He remembered being beaten.

He was on all fours, snarling. They were kicking him. He remembered gripping an ankle and hammering below a kneecap as a man bent above him. He recalled the snap and the scream. Then there was blood in his mouth and a skull in his head, splitting, and a mirror behind his eyelids,. but no reflection . . .

He licked his lips and gagged at the taste of blood. He forced his swollen eyes open.

"For nineteen years you have marked magnificent time," said the voice

41

inside his head. "In the entire sidereal abattoir there had never been another such as Vindici for the breaking of places, the killing of people, and the stopping of things—but you have failed in the only job that really meant anything to a man you once were—" His memory licked, like the tape recordings which had filled nearly half the life of his mind, changing channels.

"You are a naked, useless man, a pitiful, crawling worm, a fork of stripped willow, a poor player, strutting and fretting—you signify nothing!—only deeds redeem, and you cannot do them!

You are afraid to look in a mirror and view the countenance of cowardice . . . !"

He snarled.

He threw his head back and bellowed through broken teeth. The pain in his wide-stretched limbs was enormous. His cry beat upon the bars and his cracked ribs and was broken in mid-howl. He sobbed within his cage.

His wrists and ankles were clamped tight against the frame of the great rack. There was shade below, but the hot light of the sun drove needles through his eyeballs.

He looked about, slowly.

He was alone, at the bottom of a pit, with his rack. An ugly *dejá vu* occurred as a coffin swam through his mind, drifting in a lake of blood.

The walls were stone, and at least twenty feet high. They were unbroken by any openings. The enclosure was about ten feet square. His rack was tilted back at a ninety-degree angle. The mouth of the pit was open.

It was too high, too smooth to climb, even if he could manage to break his metal bonds.

The sun was a green one-spot on a pale blue die, slightly right of center. Nothing intruded upon his view of the heavens, not even a cloud.

He cursed the sun, he cursed the day. He cursed the gods shooting craps above him.

*

The sun moved directly to the center of its square, then began an amoeba-like crawling to the left. Finally, it kissed the rim of the pit. He expected it to dissolve and flow down the wall, raining green fire upon him. Instead, it was sliced shorter and shorter and finally was gone. The square became an empty aquarium.

Voices.

"There he is," said the woman.

"Is he still alive?"

He tilted his head and looked up, hating.

"Lord! Look at those muscles! Those eyes—!"

"He's a halfy," said her companion, a thin youth with a bandage about his head. "I'm going to come back every hour. I'm going to watch him die. But he still has a lot of life left—halfies are strong."

The woman waved at him, jauntily.

"Halfy!" cried the boy. "You failed. My father is getting better and he's going to live! He'll personally open your veins as soon as he's able to move!"

Vindici's eyes burned and the boy reeled. He began to fall forward. The woman grabbed his arm and jerked him back.

"It didn't work," he called down. "Nice try, though. Your daughter is better at that sort of thing! I hope you're around to see what I'm going to do with her."

"The ingredients of tiger soup are hard to come by . . . " groaned the man on the rack.

There was laughter above.

"But we've caught the tiger!"

The square grew empty once more, and the sounds trailed off in the distance.

Daughter. They had said "daughter," hadn't they? Yes. Ramsay's daughter. Cassy . . .

—Cassy. Where are you?

—Hiding. In the apartment building. There is a room—dark, cool. It was not in the blueprints.

—They are looking for you now. Do not leave the place.

—Where are you?

—It is not important.

—I see a piece of sky. A window?

He closed his eyes.

—No.

—You are hurting. But I thought you were dead.

—Don't worry about me. Stay safe. Leave this world when things grow still once more.

—Where is there to go?

—Offworld, anywhere.

—The Federation will be everywhere. I am of Turner's world, not of man's. So are you.

—No! I am Vindici! I was not born!

Silence.

—Why are you weeping, girl?

—How could you tell? I was weeping for my father.

—Remsay is dead. He was weak.

—No. You are Ramsay. Vindici is facade and falsehood.

—Go away!

Silence.

*

Night. Clouds.

Stars, and the sounds of birds.

In the El Greco sky, framed by lips of the pit, nine stars were arrow awaiting target . . . .

A head interrupted the sky.

. . . Bandaged head, white. Halo of steel, crown . . . . Mock of steel, laughter . . . .

"We know where she is, Vindici! I'll have her here and let you watch soon!"

Emptied crown. Clouds. Seas of cotton.

—Run! Run! They know where you are!

—How could they?

—I do not know.
Flight before fury.

*

Harrison hurried through the night, a puzzled look on his tired face, a gun in his pocket, and Stat's latest pronouncement rolling about his head like a marble in a tin can.

*

Youth's the season made for Joy—
Richard perspired as the nine metal-blue eyes peered pyramid through his skylight.

He tried to raise an arm, but both were clamped to the bed.

"The world of Stat's a drunken bat . . . "

Smythe poured another drink.

" . . . Only Statcom knows," he hiccupped.

MINUS TWO

You're a fool, Vindici! Take a good look!" He pushed her forward.

Cassy?

–Yes. They were waiting.

"You flushed your cub for us! Tomorrow morning my father will be able to sit up! He's going to kill you then! But tonight is mine—and hers!"

I'm sorry, Cassy.

–You didn't know. They tricked you.

"I knew you halfies could talk, mind to mind! You made her run!—Into my arms!"

Vindici roared. It was not a human sound that emerged from his stiffened throat. The hackles rose on the back of his neck.

His eyes became distinguishable to those above him. Two burning points . . . .

She tilted her head, straining against her captors grip.

I love you.

As she moved, her net of tiger gold snared the formation of mine, and drew it, wreath, to her brow.

There was a snapping sound and Vindici's left hand came free. The pain in his right wrist increased to unbearable proportions. His voice rose and fell through a terrible series of wails and cries.

Laughter above, and an empty canvas . . .

Words from everywhere seemed to be saying, "Come back! I hate you!" to everyone in the palace and on the grounds.

Richard moaned within his prison of pipettes.

Vindici looked up at the nine starships, then dropped his head.

"One time were you peerless," said the tape-worn synapses. "Once the arm of Tamburlaine was invincible, and the dagger of Vindici never missed its mark. Under all the passes of Time's wand only one remained—you, Vindici!—of the ancient dynasty of bloodletters. Mad in Argos, you slew your mother, tongueless in Castile, you stabbed Lorenzo —you, the lance of the black Quixote, dagger of the damned, cup of hemlock, dart of Loki—the bough where the murderer hangs . . . . "

"I still am," he muttered.

"No, you are a man on a rack, a broken blade, a gob of flesh and phlegm . . . . "

"Yes! You are a snapped firing-pin, an unvoiced battle-cry—you are the want of a horseshoe for which a kingdom was 'lost . . . . '"

A mirror appeared before his eyes.

"No!" he cried. "No! I am Vindici! The son of Death! Bred in the Senecan twilight of Jacobean demigods, and punctual as death!"

He looked into the mirror.

"Behold!" he laughed. "Behold I am the fury!"

Vindici, the tiger, sprang.

*

All went black as the world carne to an end.

*

Dribble.

Dribble.

Rain. Soft on lips of sand.

A moan.

. . . Dribble.

*

"Water," he asked. "Water."

"Here."

48

"More."

"Here."

"Good. More."

"Slowly. Please."

Green met green in circles of seeing.

"Here?" she asked.

"Here," he nodded.

"Father."

"Cassy."

He looked at the world.

"What happened?"

"Gone. Dead. Rest now. Talk later."

"Richard?"

"Dead."

"Larry?"

"Dead."

"The ships?"

"Only Vindici knows."

He slept.

Nine starships waiting. Hurry, hurry, hurry . . . .

MINUS ONE

It is morning," she said, "and no birds are singing—all of them dead, and fallen from the trees."

"Vindici always hated the birds," he told her. "Where are the soldiers? The courtiers?"

"All of them dead."

He propped himself on an elbow.

"'Paraphysical conversion from a psychopath neurosis,'" he repeated, "'produced when the stimuli overwhelm available physical responses.' —Channing's words never meant anything to Vindici, but I remember them."

"And the battle conches? Nine starships?"

He snapped his fingers and winced at the pain in his wrist.

"Gone. Dust—dust of dust. He blacked them."

He dropped back to the grass.

"Everyone," he said.

"Every living thing in the palace and on the grounds," she agreed, "except for me."

"Even himself."

Ramsay looked at the sky.

"How classic and dreadful. What a man he was!"

"Man? Are you sure?"

"No, I'm not. I couldn't do it." Harrison entered the open gates and moved through the orchard.

He approached the couple on the lawn.

"Good morning."

"Good morning."

"Quiet here."

"Yes."

He looked about.

"How did you get him up?"

"The same winch they used to lower him. I put it back in the shed." She pointed.

"Neat, aren't you?"

She gave her father another drink.

Harrison jammed his hands into his pockets and paced out a square.

"What did you do with the ships?"

She shrugged.

"He says Vindici 'blocked' them."

He stared at the man on the ground.

"Vindici . . ."

"Ramsay," corrected the split lips.

"That makes it harder."

He removed the gun from his pocket.

"I'm sorry, honestly. But it has to be done."

"'The bird-killer weeps,' said the sparrow. 'Watch his hands, not his eyes,' answered the crow."

"Stat says Vindici must die."

"He *is* dead," she told him.

He shook his head.

"So long as he breathes, the tiger lives—and he might appear again someday."

"No," "No," said Ramsay.

"I'm sorry."

He raised the gun. He aimed for a long, long while.

Slowly, he toppled forward onto his face.

Cassiopeia smiled.

"Family heritage."

She picked up his gun and tossed it into the pit.

"He'll have a sore nose this afternoon."

She helped her father to his feet, and together they staggered toward the unguarded vehicle pens.

*

Harrison was right," he told her, "he's not dead."

He drew the smoke deep into his lungs and exhaled heavily.

"What do you mean?"

"I'm both now. We've fused. I know what he knew."

"Everything?"

"Including the hate," he said.

"What's there left to hate?" she asked, almost eagerly.

"Stat."

"What good does hating Stat do you? Stat's like Time—it just goes on and on."

He shook his head.

"There is a difference. Stat must come to an end."

"How's it to be done?"

He stared into the small mirror by the bedstead.

"I can't black it, like he did the ships. That calls for a special kind of hate, and I can't muster it. But there's enough of the tiger left in me for another hunt."

He closed his eyes.

"I do know how to get to Stat. Harrison is alive. When he reports failure it will only be a matter of time before Stat finds another way. I'll die then."

"If Stat could be destroyed . . . " her voice trailed off. "If only Stat could be destroyed! It used you, me, everyone!"

She looked back at him.

"Nine battle conches couldn't break the Federation."

"Not with Stat and Vindici on their side," he answered. "But if the tiger decapitates the robot and disappears, then the out-worlds might declare their independence and have a chance of maintaining it."

"What will you need?"

"Nothing. All the tools of my trade are cached in the hills."

"You can't leave in your condition."

"I'll be in shape by the time I get there—shape enough. It's a long walk home from heaven, even with h.d."

She mixed him a drink and watched him drink it.

That afternoon, upon a hilltop, she purred softly as he leapt into the sky screaming fire, to hunt the drunken bat.

*

Thirty minutes before Stat came to an end the ship's radio blared.

"Identify! Identify! These lanes are off-limits to civilian traffic! Identify!"

Smythe watched through a beacon-eye that peered from an island of rock. He pressed a button.

"Bring Channing—fast!"

Spaghettis of paper coiled about his ankles. He raised a strand, then dropped it.

He switched off the automatic warnings and picked up a microphone.

"The ship has been identified, Vindici. It's ours, You know."

He lifted the toggle and waited.

No reply.

He spoke again.

"Statcom predicted that if you survived you would try to return. Stat cannot be destroyed."

The door sighed open and Channing stood blinking at him, flanked by two maintenance robots.

"Come in, quickly!"

He entered the control room, eyes mild, face placid.

Smythe slapped him.

"Channing Doctor Karel Channing," he said. "I am Carl Smythe. You are a psychiatric engineer in the Corps d'Assassins. You created a super killer named Vindici. You have been under sedation recently, but you remember Vindici, don't you?

"Yes," said Channing, "I remember Vindici. I remember Smythe, and Channing."

"Good." He handed him the microphone. "It was your voice that conditioned Vindici. Take this and talk to him. He is outside. Tell him to answer you."

Channing gripped the microphone clumsily.

"Vindici?" he asked it. "Vindici, this is Doctor Channing. If you can hear me, answer me."

Smythe pushed up on the lever.

The talk box talked.

"Hi, Doc. Sorry I have to kill you and a lot of other people, just to knock off Stat, but that's how the story goes. You know, *Frankenstein*, et cetera."

Smythe snatched the microphone.

"Vindici, listen. We can still use you. Land. I'll open a hatch. You'll need more conditioning, but you can still be of use to Stat."

"Sorry," came the reply, "this isn't Vindici, it's Captain Ramsay of Turner's Guard. Twenty years age I declared war on the Federation. I just remembered that recently. You were a kid then—I don't know what you are now, Smythe . . . . "

"That's your last word on the matter?"

"I'm afraid so."

"Then we're going to destroy you," he said, switching on a panel of lights. "I really hate to lose a good man."

"Go ahead and try losing me," said Ramsay. "I was raised from the dead to do this job. Tell that old washing machine you have to do its worst."

*

Smythe pushed the button numbered 776.

He glanced at the screen.

The hovering ship, bearing the number 776 on its side, glowed red and became a Roman Candle.

Smythe switched off the receiver.

"All the ships bear the seeds of their own destruction," he observed.

"Doesn't everything?" asked Channing.

Smythe mopped his forehead and looked at the thermostat.

"Hot in here."

"Very."

"We're shielded. That explosion shouldn't be doing this."

"It's getting hotter."

Bells began to ring.

Statcom spoke, in tongues of paper.

"Something else is out there!" cried Smythe.

Channing leaned forward and turned on the broadcast-receive unit.

"Ramsay?" he asked.

"I read you, loud and clear."

Smythe began throwing switches. Another scene appeared on the viewer. The surface of Stat was hot. A figure in a spacesuit moved about it, dropping parcels into the hatchway pocks.

"Congratulations," said Channing, "you have exceeded my expectations."

The redhead snatched the microphone.

"What are you doing out there?"

"You didn't think I'd stick with the ship when it got this close, did you? I hooked up my suit-radio to broadcast through it while I came on ahead. Stat is beginning to die."

"Not yet," said Smythe.

He inserted a key beneath a lever and turned it. He jerked down on the lever as Channing struck him.

Lying on his back, he watched Channing stare at the blazing surface of Stat.

—*My Perseus! cried Medusa, and smouldering in stone!*

Then the fires began to subside. "Inner line of defense," he laughed. "Thermite fuses."

"The tiger," Channing whispered, "is burning bright."

*

Thirty seconds before Stat carne to an end Cassiopeia began to weep, uncontrollably. She tore off her dress and smashed all the mirrors in her apartment.

With hair of tiger gold and eyes of tiger black, she stood upon the balcony, staring across the wide, dark room of the sky, her fearful symmetries of hate.

Printed in the USA
CPSIA information can be obtained
at www.ICGtesting.com
LVHW051444150224
771945LV00002BB/259